ANIMAL
EMERGENCY

LOST
KITTEN

EMILY COSTELLO

ILLUSTRATED BY LARRY DAY

For Henry Isaac Newell

Library of Congress Catalog Card Number: 99-95487
ISBN: 0-380-81111-1

First Avon edition, 2000

AVON TRADEMARK REG. U.S. PAT. OFF. AND IN OTHER COUNTRIES, MARCA REGISTRADA,
HECHO EN U.S.A.

Visit us on the World Wide Web!
www.harperchildrens.com

• 1 •

Stella Sullivan stretched, yawned, kicked off her covers, and got out of bed. She padded across her room in her bare feet and looked out the window.

The morning sky was completely clear. Not a cloud in sight.

Stella sighed.

It hadn't rained in almost four months. May, June, July, and August. Four dry, hot months in a row. The trees behind the Sullivans' small house looked worn out—the leaves on the aspens were faded and limp. The needles on the pines were brownish-green—a shade lighter than the grass.

Even the sky looked like it could use a good bath. Instead of blue, it was a hazy gray.

Stella wondered if another fire had started the night before.

Spotty forest fires had been burning in the woods surrounding Gateway—Stella's hometown—for the past few weeks. Stella and her mother, Norma, had seen one start a few weeks earlier.

One good lightning strike. A little wind. And—

FAAUUMPH! Dozens of acres had gone up in flames.

Stella and Norma had hung around for a few hours, keeping an eye on the blaze until a crew of firefighters reached the scene.

Watching the fire spread and grow was fascinating. Almost fun. Except that Stella had been worried about the wild animals.

Norma said she shouldn't worry. Wildlife wasn't bothered much by forest fires. Norma said elk and deer and sheep moved away from the heat, flames, and smoke. Birds flew away—although sometimes they were forced to abandon a nest and some fledglings. Critters that lived underground and in the water were out of harm's way. And the buffalo would graze right next to stands of burning trees.

Stella believed her mom. Still, she was concerned about a group of gray wolves that were penned up deep in the woods. The wolves couldn't run away—they were locked in.

But the fire warden had called in a team of specialized firefighters. They'd dug a fire line around the wolves' pen. With all of the fuel around them burned up, the wolves would be safe for the rest of the summer.

Stella brushed her teeth, pulled on a pair of shorts and a sleeveless T-shirt, and hurried downstairs. Rufus, Stella's five-month-old puppy, was waiting for her in the kitchen.

"Arf!" Rufus put his front paws up against the toddler gate that kept him inside the kitchen. He panted happily as Stella opened the gate.

"Hi, sweetie!" Stella let herself in.

Rufus backed up and ran in an excited circle. "Arf! Arf! Arf!"

Stella scooped Rufus up with one hand and gave him a kiss between the eyes. He licked her cheek.

Rufus was a little dog—he weighed only about four pounds. His fur was white and shaggy. He had black eyes, a black nose, and black lips. Nobody was really sure what breed he was, but he looked a lot like a Maltese.

Stella had gotten Rufus when he was two weeks old and close to death. Someone had abandoned his entire litter at a rest stop. Stella had nursed Rufus back to health, even getting up in the middle of the night to feed him through a stomach tube.

She didn't mind the lost sleep because she had fallen in love with the puppy the first time she'd seen him—even though he had been a pretty pathetic sight.

"Arf!" Rufus gave Stella a sad, "feed-me" face.

"Don't try that," Stella said. "I know Mom already gave you breakfast."

She put Rufus down and went to the cabinet. She got out a bowl, a box of Cheerios, and a spoon. Then she went to the refrigerator and pulled out a gallon of milk.

Stella took her cereal to the table. Rufus settled in at her feet, sighing.

Even though it was only eight-thirty, the house was quiet. Stella's father was off at Montana State University where he was teaching Introduction to Journalism in summer school. Stella's fourteen-year-old sister, Cora, had gone to her job at Jake's Stables. Norma was already at work.

Norma had been putting in long hours lately.

Summers were always crazy at Goldenrock National Park, where Norma worked as a wildlife biologist. Thousands of people—throngs really—descended on the place from across the United States and the world. Norma kept busy giving lectures about the creatures that lived in the park—buffalo, bighorn sheep, bald eagles, bats, bears, and hundreds more.

When she wasn't giving lectures, Norma was answering tourists' questions—lots of them. Most of the questions were about the park's animals. But there were a few questions like these: Where is the nearest bathroom? Are there poisonous

snakes in the woods? Have you seen a six-year-old boy who looked lost?

Lately, Norma had also been answering lots of questions about forest fires. She called this part of her job "impersonating Smoky Bear."

Stella spooned up the last of her cereal. She put her bowl on the floor. Rufus licked the bowl.

After she cleaned up, Stella got Rufus's brush out of a drawer. She pulled the little dog onto her lap and started brushing his silky hair. Under his neck. Down his back.

Rufus wiggled under the brush. He leaned gently into bristles, panting happily. When Stella paused to clean the brush, he stood up as straight as possible on her knees and waited patiently for her to continue.

Stella laughed. "You're such a show-off," she said. "You know you're adorable, don't you?"

Rufus nudged the brush with his nose.

"Don't worry, I'm not finished yet."

The phone rang.

Stella put Rufus down on the couch.

"Arf!"

"Just a minute. Let me get the phone." Stella picked up the receiver. "Hello?"

"Stella? It's Cora."

Stella's heart skipped. Cora's voice was all wrong.

"I need to talk to Dad," Cora said urgently.

"What's wrong?"

"Haven't you heard? A fire—a big one. It's heading this way. We just got a call from the fire warden. We've got to evacuate the stables. I . . . I need to talk to Dad," she repeated.

"Cora, it's Wednesday. Dad's in Billings."

"Wednesday? Oh, Stella . . . Jake isn't here. Someone important came in. A politician, I think. Jake wanted to lead her tour personally. He—he left me in charge."

Stella suddenly felt more alert. They had to evacuate the stables. Twenty horses. No, that wasn't right. Some of the horses would be out with Jake. Still, there'd be a lot.

"I'll come help," Stella said, trying to stay calm.

"Okay. But hurry."

The phone went dead.

Stella hung up. She stopped and thought for a minute, looking down at herself. Shorts weren't the right thing to wear to a fire.

Taking the steps two at a time, Stella ran up to her room and changed into a pair of long pants and a long-sleeved shirt. She pulled on a pair of boots and then pounded down the stairs.

Stella's running around excited Rufus. He circled her, barking and jumping up on her leg. Rufus clearly thought that Stella was going to take him for a walk or swimming or somewhere exciting. Stella felt bad, but she knew Rufus needed to stay home. He'd only get in the way at the stables. And she didn't want him to get hurt.

"Come here, you." Stella picked up the excited puppy, backed into the kitchen, and closed the toddler gate. She put him down next to his water dish.

Rufus trotted happily after Stella—until he realized she was trying to sneak out the kitchen door without him.

"Ruf! Ruf, ruf, ruf, ruf!"

Stella felt a flash of impatience. She needed to hurry, and Rufus wasn't helping.

"Stop making so much noise," she said crossly. "I'll be right back. We can play then."

"Rufrufruf!"

"Rufus—hush!"

Stella's angry tone made Rufus lower his head. But he didn't back away from the door. Stella had to close it slowly and carefully to keep from squashing the tip of his nose.

Stella pulled her bike out of the shed. She hopped on and headed down the road, away from town.

Jake's Stables was not that far from the Sullivans' house. Just a couple of miles down the road, past half a dozen small motels and campgrounds, to the edge of Goldenrock.

As Stella pedaled closer, she noticed that the haze was getting thicker. She turned into the driveway to the stables and stopped for a second to stare.

Flames.

Stella saw towering red and yellow flames that shot up a story or two. They'd engulfed the pine stand that backed into Jack's horse barn.

And that wasn't all. A burning limb had broken off a tree and smashed into the barn's roof.

The shingles on the roof were wood. Stella watched as the wind gusted and a line of flames raced across the shingles.

Were the horses still in there?

Stella pushed off, pedaling her bike as fast as possible. When she got closer, she saw a group of kids who were around Cora's age. They were gathered around a mare.

"Is she hurt?" Stella called, dropping her bike and running toward them.

One of the girls turned toward Stella. She pushed a lock of brown hair off her forehead. Her face was pale, drawn. "I think Rae's leg is broken. She panicked in the fire and went wild."

Rae. Stella remembered Cora talking about this horse. She was the gentlest mare at the stables. They always put little kids on her.

"Did you call my Aunt Anya?" Anya was the local vet. Stella was her unofficial helper. She spent as much time as possible at her aunt's animal clinic because she wanted to be a vet when she grew up.

"Cora did. She's on her way."

"Where *is* Cora?"

The girl pointed toward the barn.

Stella felt a cold spurt of fear in her chest. Did Cora know that the barn was about to go up in flames? She had to warn her.

Stella ran closer. "Cora! Cora!"

No answer.

Stella could hear something, though. It was a few seconds before she realized it was the horses. They were huffing for air and nickering loudly.

They sounded afraid. Goose bumps popped out on Stella's arms. What was going on in there?

"Cora! Cora!"

No answer.

Stella rushed toward the stable. She opened the enormous wooden door.

She had to save Cora.

She had to save the horses.

• 2 •

moke.

Thick smoke.

Stella squinted, her eyes burning. Where was Cora? The smoke made it hard to see. Even with the door wide open, the inside of the stable was dim.

"Cora!" Taking in enough air to yell meant sucking in some serious smoke. Stella started to cough.

Cora didn't answer.

The fire itself gave off some light. But the flames flickered and wavered, throwing uneven shadows. Not much help.

Flames were tearing apart the back of the stable. Stella could hear boards snapping and the floor creaking. Somewhere nearby a horse was noisily blowing out air.

"I'm coming," Stella whispered.

She was scared. Her knees were Jell-O. She wanted to turn around and run back outside for help. But that was no good. The kids outside were busy with Rae.

She inched forward through the gloom until she felt a latch. The first stall door. A horse was inside. She could hear his hooves hitting against the wooden door. Working by feel, she lifted the little metal bar and swung the door open.

Fa-rump! Fa-rump!

The horse came galloping out, tossing his head. Stella could see the whites of his eyes, but not much else.

Stella scrambled to get out of the way. She backed up too fast and stumbled, fighting to regain her footing.

OUUFFF!

The horse plowed into her. She fell backward, landing hard on her back. The impact knocked the breath out of her. She gasped, but her lungs refused to fill with air.

The horse reared. "Nee-he-he-he!" he snorted.

Stella looked up. The horse's hooves were heading straight for her! She wiggled to the side.

FA-RUMP!

One of the horse's hooves landed inches from her shoulder. There was a flash of darkness and a musty smell. Then the stallion was past her, running toward the door.

Stella took a deep breath. The air was clearer near the ground. *I'll stay low,* she thought.

She lay still for a moment, listening to her heart thump. Then she crawled toward the burning side of the barn. At the next stall, she reached up, opened a latch, and quickly scrambled back against the wall. A horse came huffing out and made a quick left toward the stable door. *Good,* Stella thought. *They remember their way out.*

This wasn't going to be too hard. Stella began to crawl toward the next stall.

FA-RUMP! FA-RUMP! FA-RUMP!

Stella jerked back against the wall.

A horse came galloping wildly toward her. And then—swish! It was past.

Where did she come from? Stella wondered. It took her a second to figure it out. Someone else was setting the horses free.

Cora.

"Cora!" Stella hollered.

No answer. Where was she? Stella couldn't see her in the aisle.

Stella crawled forward and reached up to unlock another stall. She braced herself against the wall—expecting the sound of crashing hooves. None came.

Was the stall empty?

Stella crawled cautiously forward and peered

inside. She immediately recognized the horse—it was Cinnamon, the quarter horse Cora rode in barrel-racing competitions.

Cinnamon was hovering way in the back of her stall, staring fearfully toward the aisle. Her nostrils were flared, and her ears were plastered against her head.

"Hi, sweetie," Stella murmured, doing her best to keep her voice calm.

Cinnamon was a nervous horse. That was part of what made her so good in competition. But now Stella needed Cinnamon to be brave.

"Let's go outside and get some fresh air." Stella stood up and quietly approached Cinnamon. She ran a hand down the mare's sweaty neck. The horse had one wide-open eye fixed on her. Stella could hear her tail swishing nervously back and forth.

Without warning, Stella gave Cinnamon a firm smack on the haunch. "Yah! Yah!"

Cinnamon startled. But instead of running toward the door, she skittered farther into the corner of her box.

Now what? Stella asked herself.

Cinnamon wasn't wearing a bridle, so Stella didn't have any way of leading her out of the stall. She looked around for something to use, and spotted a length of rope hanging on the side of the box.

Stella pulled the rope down and tied it into a loop. She slipped the loop into Cinnamon's mouth and behind her ears. Then she ran the rope under Cinnamon's neck and tied another loose knot.

"Come on, girl," Stella said. "Let's get out of here." She pulled gently on the rope. Cinnamon took a slow, hesitant step.

Stella pulled a little harder. "Come on, it's okay. I won't let anything hurt you."

Another step.

Another.

Now Stella was standing just at the edge of the aisle. Her eyes stung. She couldn't get her breath. Couldn't stop coughing.

The smoke was much thicker.

Stella's heart started to thump, thump. She had been worried about getting Cinnamon out of the barn. Now she started to wonder if she could get *herself* out.

Cinnamon sensed Stella's fear. She pulled back on the rope. Stella squinted through the smoke. She saw the horse rearing back, showing her teeth. Panicking.

"It's okay!" Stella yelled.

Cinnamon yanked the rope out of Stella's grasp. She backed into her stall, nickering.

"No," Stella moaned. "Don't do that. Please." She tried to think of another way to encourage

Cinnamon, and came up with nothing. She felt light-headed. Like this was all a bad dream.

She felt like sitting down on the floor. Just resting.

Crrr . . .

Stella slowly turned toward the sound coming from the back of the barn.

Crracckkk!

A beam smashed to the ground, sending sparks flying. The roof in that part of the stable sagged down. Suddenly the air inside the barn seemed much hotter. Breathing dried out Stella's mouth, her throat. Even her lungs felt dry.

It was definitely time to go.

But Stella couldn't leave without Cinnamon.

And Cinnamon wasn't budging.

3

"**S**tella!" Cora raced down the aisle, leading two horses. Her face was wet with sweat, her hair slick with it. "What . . . are you . . . doing here?" she gasped.

"Cinnamon . . . won't . . . come." Breathing was almost impossible. Talking, too.

Cora took something out from under her arm and tossed it at Stella. A rough blanket. The kind stable hands use to keep horses warm.

"Put this . . . over . . . her eyes."

Stella unfolded the blanket. She took two steps in the stall and tossed it over Cinnamon's head. The horse's head drooped, but she didn't shake off the blanket. Stella grabbed her rope and pulled. Cinnamon stepped forward.

"Let's go!" Cora said.

First Cora and the two horses. Then Stella and

Cinnamon. Stella's lungs were burning. Her eyes were stinging. She knew the barn door was only a few yards away. But she wasn't sure if she'd make it. Stumbling. Gasping. Half blind.

Cinnamon was following the other horses. All Stella had to do was hold onto the rope, and follow her.

With each step, the air got cooler. The smoke thinned. Stella felt her head clearing. And then . . .

"Stella! Cora!"

They were outside. Blinking in the sunlight. The driveway was a swirl of frantic activity. People running back and forth and loading horses into trailers. Someone taking photographs.

Rrrrwww-wow! WOW! WOW! A bright yellow fire truck came screaming into the drive. Another followed closely behind. Firefighters started to hop off the trucks.

Stella dropped Cinnamon's rope and sank to her knees. She coughed, breathed, coughed, breathed. Someone handed her a cup of water and she swallowed it down. Slowly she started to feel more normal. To become aware that she was surrounded by people. She lifted her head.

Anya was kneeling right in front of her. She did not look the least little bit happy. Her usually merry eyes were dark. Her mouth was turned down in a scowl.

"Aunt Anya," Stella said. "What's the matter?"

"What's the matter?" Anya shouted. "The matter is that I just saw you and Cora run out of a burning stable! Which makes me strongly suspect you ran *into* a burning stable sometime in the not-too-distant past!"

"Oh." Stella didn't know what else to say.

"What were you girls thinking?" Anya demanded. "You could have been killed!"

All Stella could do was stare. She'd seen her aunt in all sorts of difficult and frightening situations—examining rodeo bulls, operating on beloved pets, treating race horses worth millions of dollars. And never in all that time had Stella seen Anya lose her cool.

Until now.

Stella turned to Cora, who had collapsed on

the ground next to her. She was staring after the horses in a sort of trance. Her eyes were red and irritated. Strands of her dark hair clung to her cheeks. The cheek facing Stella was smudged with dirt.

Cora didn't look too good.

Anya was angry.

Stella suddenly realized what a crazy thing she had done. Run into a burning stable. Not too bright. Stupid, actually.

Stella was embarrassed. Her Aunt Anya always treated her with respect, trusted her to do things that could be dangerous if she wasn't careful. Now she'd shown Anya that she didn't deserve that respect.

"I—I'm sorry," Stella said. "I didn't think."

Anya frowned. "How do you feel now? Lightheaded? Short of breath?"

"No," Stella said.

Cora shook her head. She was still staring off into the distance.

"Any burns?" Anya demanded.

"No."

"Skin looks normal. Do you know what day it is?"

"Wednesday," Stella said.

"A Wednesday in July," Cora added. "I don't know the date."

"So you're feeling disoriented?"

Cora smiled. "Aunt Anya, I *never* know the date in the middle of the summer. I'm fine. No burns, broken bones, or bru—"

Crrrraaa—BAM!

Another beam in the roof let loose. The stable started to fall in on itself as the fire completely engulfed it.

"Whoa," Stella said.

Anya shuddered. "Another few minutes, and you guys wouldn't have gotten out of there."

Stella hated having Anya mad at her. She wanted to explain. "We were just trying to save the horses."

Anya's expression softened. "I know," she said. "But you went too far."

A firefighter came running toward them. "Anyone hurt?"

Anya stood up. "They're fine," she called back.

"Good," the firefighter called. "You folks will have to get out of here. Pronto!"

Behind him, a group of firefighters was hauling a massive hose toward the stable. They braced themselves as the hose suddenly filled with a powerful burst of water.

Cora stood up and pulled Stella to her feet.

"Let's go, let's go, let's go!" the firefighter yelled.

"What about the horses?" Cora asked, suddenly businesslike. "I can't leave until I know they've all been loaded."

Several horse trailers had already pulled onto the road. Cinnamon was being loaded into the last one. They watched as a skinny, strong-looking rancher closed the trailer doors.

"Is that all of them?" Cora called to him.

"We counted fourteen altogether."

"Jake owns twenty horses," Cora said.

"Some are in the park," Stella reminded her sister. "On the ride with Jake."

Cora's expression relaxed a tiny bit. "Right. Jake took five horses. But we're still missing one." She looked ready to run back into the stable.

Anya put a hand on Cora's shoulder. "Cora, we have them all. When I got here, one of the mares had a badly broken leg."

"Rae."

"Yes, Rae. I had to put her down."

Cora's face dropped. She covered her face with her hands. "Noooo," she moaned.

Anya pulled her into a hug. "Honey, I'm so sorry. But it really was the best thing for Rae. That leg was never going to heal."

The firefighter jogged up to them. "You folks have to leave. Don't make me tell you again."

Anya nodded and let go of Cora. "Okay, let's go. We need to get the horses settled at the fairgrounds."

Cora nodded. Her eyes were flooded with tears.

Stella took Cora's hand and gave it a squeeze. She felt sad, too.

Anya's 4x4 was parked on the edge of the pasture. Cora crawled into the middle of the seat. Anya gave Stella a concerned look as she opened the back.

Stella shook her head. Poor Rae. Poor Cora.

Anya helped Stella load the bikes into the truck. They climbed into the cab. Anya pulled out onto the road right after the trailer with Cinnamon in the back.

Stella turned around. The firefighters had two big hoses aimed at the barn. But it was already too late. The stable was beyond saving.

"Jake is going to need a new stable," Stella said, feeling even worse. She knew how much her sister loved that stable. About as much as Stella loved the animal clinic.

"At least we got all of the horses out," Anya said quickly.

"That's the important thing," Stella said.

Cora nodded solemnly.

Everyone was quiet as Anya drove the rest of the way through town, heading toward the fairgrounds on the east side.

The five horse trailers from the stables had pulled up. They were parked next to several big rigs that Stella guessed carried livestock from the ranches near Jake's.

About a dozen people were milling around. An official from the fairgrounds was telling people where the animals would be housed. Apparently a plan had been drafted long ago, just in case.

Stella, Anya, and Cora climbed out of the 4x4 just as Jake galloped up on a big gray stallion. The horse was breathing hard, and Jake dismounted practically before it came to a stop.

"Cora! Are you okay?"

"Yes." That one word came out sounding slightly shaky.

"The other stable hands?"

"They're fine."

Jake was still for a moment. "How many did we lose?"

Cora's eyes flooded with tears again. "Um—Rae broke her leg and we—Anya had to put her down."

Jake wrapped a hairy arm around Cora's shoulder. "Don't cry," he said gruffly. "You did good. One loss . . . they told me the stable is completely destroyed. I couldn't have done a better job myself."

Cora gave Jake a teary smile. "Thanks."

"I should be the one saying thanks."

Cora wiped her eyes. "Stella helped."

"And practically got herself killed," Anya added. She still sounded cross.

Jake's smile faded. "How so?"

"These girls went into the stable to release the horses," Anya told him. "They got out about a minute before the place collapsed."

"What?" Jake's face turned an alarming shade of red. He took a step away from Cora and pointed a finger in her face. "You're fired!"

Cora's mouth dropped open. "But Jake . . ."

"You never, never should have gone into that barn! You could have been killed."

Cora sighed. "I know that now! Everyone keeps telling me. But I bet you would have done the same thing."

Jake and Anya exchanged looks.

"Okay, you're not fired," Jake said quietly. "But please, please be more sensible in the future."

"Promise," Cora said sullenly.

"Yo, Jake! Could you sign this, please?" The fairground official waved him over.

Jake gave Cora a quick pat on the head. "See you later." He jogged off.

Anya's cell phone bleeped. "Hello? Jack—hey." Anya took a few steps away from them to continue her conversation.

Cora rolled her eyes at Stella. "I wonder if Dad is going to yell at us, too."

"Probably," Stella said. "But I think you're a hero. If you hadn't done something, all those horses would have died. The firefighters got there too late to help."

Cora smiled. "I think you're a hero, too."

Stella felt good. Cora was five years older than she was. She knew how to do just about everything better than Stella did. Which meant Cora didn't go around telling Stella how great she was all the time. It felt nice.

Anya headed toward them. "Your dad heard about the fire on the radio. He's on his way home. He wants you to meet him there."

"Are we in trouble?" Stella asked.

Anya shrugged. "I told him what happened."

"We're in trouble," Cora said.

"Don't keep your dad waiting," Anya said.

Stella felt like she was going to her doom. Not that Jack had a bad temper. He'd probably just give them a "you really disappointed me" lecture. But still. It wouldn't be fun.

The girls got their bikes out of the 4x4, and slowly rode back through town. Everyday life was going on as usual. Tourists were strolling along with ice cream cones. People were loading groceries into their trucks.

Wait . . . maybe everything wasn't quite normal.

Stella spotted a couple of men standing on the corner in front of the hardware store. A huge pile of gear was next to them. Duffels. Backpacks. Toolboxes. Stella glimpsed some writing on one of the bags: MISSOULA SMOKEJUMPERS.

Smokejumpers are firefighters trained to fight

remote forest fires. They got to them by parachuting out of airplanes. Norma had been a smokejumper for a few years while she was in graduate school. It was the smokejumpers who had saved the wolves.

But why were they here now?

The fire at the stables wasn't way out in the woods. Maybe the smokejumpers were here for another fire. Or maybe the fire near town was bigger than Stella thought.

Cora and Stella turned onto Route 2A, heading out of town. The wind gusted up, and Stella suddenly got a whiff of smoke. Was that coming from the air? Or off her clothes?

Stella looked out at the distant mountains. She felt as if she were seeing them through a gauzy curtain. Had the haze been so heavy this morning? Stella didn't think so.

"What's that?" Cora asked.

Stella slowed her bike. Up ahead was a row of plastic orange traffic cones. Behind the cones was a line of blue wooden barricades. Stella had seen the barricades before. The police used them to mark parade routes through town.

A couple of police officers were standing in front of the barricade, talking to some people in a camper with California license plates.

"There's Assistant Sheriff Rose," Stella said. "Let's ask her what's going on."

The girls started to steer their bikes around the barricade.

Sheriff Rose came up to them. "Sorry, girls. I can't let you through."

"Why not?" Cora asked.

"Forest fire heading this way. We're evacuating the west side of town. Clearing out this whole valley."

Stella felt as if someone had punched her in the stomach. Hard. "Is our house on fire?"

"No, no," Sheriff Rose said. "Don't worry. This is just a precaution. If any of the houses *do* burn, we want everyone out."

The girls exchanged looks. So it was possible that their house was in danger. Now what?

"The Red Cross is setting up a shelter at the high school," Sheriff Rose told them. "You might want to meet up with your folks there."

"Mom's shift doesn't end until eight," Stella said.

"Has our dad been here?" Cora asked.

"Haven't seen him."

Cora thought for a moment. "He's on his way home from Billings," she told Sheriff Rose. "He should be here in about half an hour. Could you tell him we went to Aunt Anya's?"

"Will do," Sheriff Rose said.

"Come on," Cora said to Stella. "Let's go."

Something was nagging at Stella. Some reason she had to get home. . . .

Rufus!

"Cora," Stella said. "Rufus is locked in the kitchen!"

• 4 •

"What?" Cora said. "We have to get him! If the house catches on fire . . ."

"I know," Stella said.

The girls turned to face Assistant Sheriff Rose. Stella was sure Rose would understand. She knew Rufus. She was the one who had found him abandoned at that rest stop. Rufus would have died if Sheriff Rose hadn't rescued him.

"We have to go back to our house," Stella said. "Rufus is locked inside."

Assistant Sheriff Rose started to shake her head.

"But it will only take me two minutes!" Stella's voice was rising as she started to panic. "I won't even go into the house. I'll just open the door, grab Rufus, and come right back."

Sheriff Rose took a deep breath. She looked sad. "Sorry, Stella. Can't do it."

Stella felt tears spring to her eyes. "Please?"

"Please?" Cora chimed in.

"Sorry." Sheriff Rose sounded more firm this time. Another car pulled up, and she went to talk to the driver.

Stella bit her lip. She didn't understand why Sheriff Rose was being so strict. If the fire wasn't close to her house, what was the big deal?

Maybe she should sneak into the valley. She could get to the house through the woods—just hike in a big U around the barricade.

Stella felt guilty almost as soon as the thought formed. Hadn't she just promised Anya that she wouldn't take any more risks? Sneaking around the barricade was the wrong thing to do.

Unless . . .

Maybe Sheriff Rose wasn't telling them the truth. Maybe the house *was* burning.

A powerful image flooded Stella's mind. Little Rufus, alone in the kitchen. Watching the room fill with smoke. Barking for someone to let him out. Barking for Stella.

Stella took a shaky breath. "Cora . . . we have to do *something*."

Cora put a hand on her back. "Um, okay. Listen, let's head into town and talk to Anya. Maybe the police will let her through."

"Okay," Stella agreed.

They turned their bikes around and headed

back into town. Things seemed different now. Like a state of emergency had invaded Gateway's Main Street in the past ten minutes.

A flood of trucks and cars was causing a traffic jam. The sidewalks were crowded, too—mostly with groups of people standing around talking uneasily.

The girls slowed as they rode past the high school. The parking lot was half full. Two big Red Cross trucks were parked right in front of the entrance. People carrying back packs and sleeping bags were lining up to get in.

Stella was reminded of a movie she'd seen earlier that summer. In the movie, an asteroid was heading for Earth. Everyone in Los Angeles had to flee, and naturally they got caught in a massive traffic jam.

The creepy thing was . . . this wasn't a movie. This was real life. Main Street, Gateway. Stella felt a strange sense of disbelief. But she could feel the sticky handles of her bike and the sun beating down on her head. This definitely wasn't a dream.

They kept going—riding faster now.

Anya's truck was pulled up onto the grass in front of the animal clinic. The street was lined with cars. The clinic's front door was open, and people were sitting on the steps.

"What's going on?" Stella asked.

"Let's find out."

The girls dumped their bikes behind the clinic and hurried inside. Anya was in the waiting room, holding a yellow pad and talking to an elderly man with a tired-looking beagle on a leash. He was the first person in a long line.

"Aunt Anya?" Stella said.

Anya turned to them. "Girls—where did you come from?"

"Our street is barricaded."

"Where's your dad?"

"Probably caught in traffic," Cora said. "Do you need some help?"

"Do I ever! I just got back here about ten minutes ago, and all of these people were waiting."

"The Red Cross won't accept pets," the elderly man explained.

"Most of these people want to board animals," Anya said. "Stella, you know the drill. We need them to fill out a boarding form and a blue card for their pet's cage."

Stella hesitated. Anya needed help. And so did all of these people and their pets. But it was hard for her to think about anything but saving Rufus.

"What can I do?" Cora asked.

"Why don't you pass out boarding forms to the people who are waiting?" Anya said. "Go into my office and look for some extra pens. Stella, you can get the animals settled. Things are going to get crowded, so use all the available space—including my apartment and outside."

"Okay," Stella said. She decided to ask Anya about Rufus as soon as things got organized.

Stella took the beagle's leash and led him into the backyard. The dog run already had a dachshund and a dalmatian in it.

"It's going to get crowded, all right," Stella said. She got a muzzle out of the supply shed and put it on the beagle. He didn't struggle. He seemed like a sweet old dog, but the muzzle was still a necessity. Strange animals often fought when you housed them together. Muzzles made the dogs much safer and Stella could see that the dachshund and dalmatian were already wearing them.

After the beagle was settled, Stella went back inside. Anya handed her a parakeet in a fancy silver cage. Birds like a little privacy, so Stella took the cage upstairs and put it down on Anya's bedside table.

Next was another dog—a mixed breed with short legs and a very long tail. Stella put him in with the other dogs.

Back inside, she found Cora and Anya talking to Marisa Capra and her mother. Mrs. Capra looked pretty shaken up.

Marisa was one of Stella's best friends. She lived with her parents at their bed and breakfast, a comfortable little inn. It was one of the most popular places to stay on the west side of town.

West side . . .

"Marisa," Stella said. "Were you evacuated?"

Marisa nodded miserably. "The firefighters pounded on the door and said we had to hurry. We had all these guests and by the time we knocked on their room doors and explained what was happening, it was time to go."

"What happened to your animals?" Stella asked.

"We put Daisy and the other goats into Mom's truck. But we had to leave Clemmy and her piglets."

Stella could understand why. Clemmy was a seven hundred-pound sow. Not the kind of animal you could buckle into the front seat.

"Plus the horses," Mrs. Capra said. "Don't forget about the horses! I'm really worried about them."

Mrs. Capra made a hobby of worrying. But this time Stella could relate.

Mrs. Barber—the woman who lived next door to the Sullivans—pushed to the front of the line. She must have heard what they were talking about. "Anya, our animals got left behind, too."

Cora shot Stella an unhappy look. They'd spent hours playing with the Barbers' pets: Max and Martha, the golden retrievers, and Flicker, the cat.

"Rufus is still at home, too," Stella said.

"Isn't there something we can do?" Mrs. Barber asked.

"Why weren't we given more notice?" someone near the door called out.

"We can't just leave our animals behind," Mr. Francis said loudly. He owned a campground down the street from the Sullivans and had two ponies, Harold and Maude.

"The fire might get them," Marisa said.

"And even if they survive the fire, they could die of starvation," Mrs. Capra said. "Or thirst."

Anya held out one hand like a traffic cop. "Everyone, please calm down. Gateway has a plan in place for situations just like this one. It's a good plan—I know because I helped write it."

"You're going to save Clemmy?" Marisa asked.

"Not me," Anya said. "The Humane Society will be in charge of rescuing pets. A group of volunteers is probably already on their way. I haven't had time to check my messages yet."

"When will they get here?" someone demanded.

"I'm not sure," Anya admitted. "But things will move much faster if we're organized when they arrive. If you have a pet stuck in the valley, Cora and Stella will collect some information from you."

Anya ripped a piece of paper off a yellow pad. She quickly made a list of information they would need and tacked it up at the reception desk.

Cora collected the information from the Capras, Mr. Francis, and Mrs. Barber, while Stella took a rabbit back to the boarder room.

When she got back to the waiting room, her father was talking to Cora.

"Stella." Jack wrapped her into a big hug. "Muffin, I'm so glad you're okay! Anya told me about the fire at Jake's, and then our street was barricaded . . ."

"I'm fine, Daddy. But Rufus is still at the house."

"Cora told me. But don't worry. He'll be fine. He's a brave dog, even if he is a bit size-challenged."

"Daddy!"

"Just teasing," Jack said. "Listen, I talked to your mom and she's going to meet us here when she gets off work. I've got to go check on Papa Pete. Stay put. And don't go running into any more burning buildings."

"I won't."

Jack headed for the door.

A woman wearing a pink sweat suit stepped to the front of the line.

"Do you have an animal to board?" Stella asked.

"A couple that need rescuing," the woman said bravely.

"Oh . . . okay." Stella glanced down at Anya's

list. She asked the woman her name and address. She wrote down detailed directions to her house, which was a cabin tucked back in the woods. She wrote that the woman was planning to stay at the Red Cross shelter.

Stella looked at the next question on the list. "What kind of pet do you have?"

"Two Dobermans. I left them in a dog run behind my cottage."

"What are the dogs' names?"

"Honey and Sugar."

Stella smiled as she wrote down the information. Dobermans are big, powerful dogs. Who would name a Doberman Honey?

Next question. "Anything special the rescuers should know?"

"Yes. They should be careful not to frighten the dogs. Honey and Sugar are very scared of strangers."

Stella looked up to see if the woman was joking. Her expression was completely serious.

"Okay," Stella said. "I'll tell them."

The next few hours were busy. Lots of Anya's usual patients needed a place to stay. And word got around at the Red Cross shelter, too. Some people who weren't Anya's clients brought in their animals to board, dropped off strays, or showed up to request that a pet be rescued.

Anya, Cora, and Stella slowly helped everyone.

The clinic filled up with animals.

The yellow pad filled up with information. A little boy had a turtle in a shoe box under his bed. A gray-haired man with a mustache had a potbellied pig in his basement.

The waiting room slowly began to empty.

"Finally," Cora said with a sigh. "I totally have to pee."

"Me too," Anya said. "I'll go upstairs. You can go downstairs."

"Deal!"

The two of them rushed off.

Stella sat down at the reception desk and opened the yellow pad. She finally had time to do something she'd been wanting to do all afternoon.

She wrote her name and address down on the yellow pad. She put down detailed directions to her house.

Next question. DESCRIBE YOUR PET.

A small white puppy, Stella wrote.

WHAT'S YOUR PET'S NAME.

Rufus.

IS THERE ANYTHING SPECIAL THE RESCUER SHOULD KNOW?

Stella tapped the pen against the pad. Then she wrote: *Please save Rufus. We love him very much.*

·5·

AM!

The clinic door crashed open and Norma moved through it. Fast. She was carrying something big in a blue-and-white-striped beach towel.

Stella jumped up. "Mom—what do you have?"

"Where's Anya? Get her."

Norma kept moving, heading toward the nearest exam room.

"Not in there," Stella called. "It's full of cats."

Norma quickly backed up. "Where?"

"Exam two is still empty," Stella told her. "I'll get Anya."

Stella ran halfway up the steps to Anya's second-floor apartment. "Aunt Anya—Mom needs you!"

Anya appeared almost immediately. "What's she got?"

"Don't know."

They pounded downstairs together. Rushed into Exam Two. Norma was holding the animal down on the table. It was struggling, but without much energy.

Stella started toward the table. "Let me help."

"Stay back," Norma said sharply.

"Why—what is it?"

"A raccoon."

"What's the big deal?"

Anya was pulling some drugs out of one of the glass-fronted cabinets. "Raccoons can carry some very serious zoonotic diseases."

"Zoonotic?"

"Diseases that can be transmitted from animals to humans," Norma explained.

"Like rabies?" Stella asked.

"Like rabies."

Stella knew that rabies was no joke. Without medical treatment, people who got it died. Died after going insane. Getting medical treatment for the virus was no picnic either: you had to have a series of painful shots.

People who worked with wild animals got vaccinated against the disease if they were smart. Anya and Norma had both been vaccinated.

"Stella—you know better than to get near a wild animal, right?" Norma said.

"Right," Stella said. "Especially one that seems too friendly or that's slobbering." Those were both symptoms of rabies.

Norma nodded her approval.

Stella watched as Anya and Norma each pulled on a pair of heavy gloves. Norma held the raccoon while Anya unwrapped the towel.

The raccoon's face came into view. He looked around the room with intelligent black eyes, his nose twitching. His face was sweet—with mask-like black patches around his eyes and white fur above and below. He used one tiny, handlike paw to push the towel down off his shoulders.

The little guy definitely had been caught in the fire. The fur on his back was singed and soot covered the white part of his nose.

Anya peered into the raccoon's face. "He looks

alert. He's not showing any signs of unusual aggression. Not too friendly, either. I don't suspect rabies, but let's keep our guard up just to be safe."

Stella crept a bit closer.

Anya put her ear close to the raccoon's face. "He's wheezing," she said after a moment. "Sounds like he's been sucking smoke. Where did you find him?"

"Out on Potters Road," Norma explained with a smile. "One of the firefighters called the rangers' station. He'd spotted this little guy in someone's swimming pool. The house was completely destroyed."

House. Destroyed. Stella's heart skipped.

Relax, she told herself. *Potters Road is miles from our house.*

"So he found the one safe place to ride out the fire," Anya said.

"Right."

"That's pretty smart," Stella said.

"Yeah," Anya agreed. "And it makes my job easier, since I won't have to cool him off."

Anya prepared a sedative. She injected the raccoon near his back hip. After a few minutes, Stella saw the raccoon relax. Anya laid him on his side. She pulled off her heavy gloves, washed her hands, and pulled on a pair of latex gloves and a surgical mask.

"Now what?" Stella asked.

"Animals with smoke inhalation are usually dehydrated," Anya said. "We'll give him some saline. Norma, you've been hauling this little guy around. What do you think he weighs?"

"About what Stella weighed when she was a year old," Norma said. "Say, twenty pounds?"

Someone knocked on the door. Cora poked her head inside. "Some people are here with a bunch of stray animals. Is it okay to take them?"

"Sure," Anya said. "I think we can squeeze in a few more overnight guests."

"I'll help Cora," Norma offered. They went out, closing the door behind them.

Anya finished making some calculations and filled a syringe. Then she injected the saline under the raccoon's skin.

Next, Anya carefully examined the raccoon from the tip of his nose to the end of his banded tail. "Just one little burn," she reported. "There on his front paw. Stella, put on gloves and a mask. I want you to get a good look at what I'm about to do. I don't want you getting near any wild animals. But you can help treat any dogs or cats that come in with burns."

"Okay." Stella felt a surge of excitement. She loved learning stuff like this. She put on a mask and gloves and moved closer to the table.

First she helped Anya clip off the raccoon's burned whiskers.

No big deal.

Then she helped put a little antibiotic ointment around the raccoon's irritated eyes.

No big deal.

"Okay, now we need to work on that burnt paw," Anya said. "Burns get infected very easily. That's why it's best to wear a mask and glove while treating them."

Stella nodded.

"First we're going to rinse the burn with some povidone-iodine solution that I've watered down," Anya said.

"What's povi—whatever you said," Stella asked.

"It's like the stuff you spray on a scrape," Anya explained.

Anya pulled the solution into a large-dose syringe and squirted it onto the wound through a needle with a large opening. Then she filled the syringe with saline and washed the wound again. Another dose of saline. And yet another.

"Okay, now we add a little ointment and dress the wound," Anya said.

"No big deal," Stella said.

"Let's get him into the incubator and pump in some oxygen," Anya said. "His lungs don't sound too bad; but he could use some help breathing."

"Neat," Stella said. "I haven't seen you use it yet."

Anya looked excited, too. She had just purchased the incubator from the hospital in Billings. The machine was designed to keep small human babies healthy.

The incubator looked like a clear plastic box. It could be completely sealed and Anya could control the temperature, oxygen and moisture levels inside. It even had portholes Anya could stick her hands through to treat patients.

Anya laid the raccoon in the incubator and closed the top. Then she ran an oxygen-supply tube through one of the holes in the box.

"Think you can remember what to do next time?"

"Sure," Stella said. But she felt a nervous twisting in her stomach. Anya seemed to think she'd need Stella's help later. Did that mean she expected lots of animals with burns? And did that mean she expected the fire to get worse?

• 6 •

"I can't believe how many animals are here," Norma said when Stella and Anya emerged from the exam room twenty minutes later.

"They all came in since they put up the road-block," Anya said. "We're pretty disorganized."

"Well, let's get organized before any more animals arrive," Cora said.

"Check," Anya said. She was carrying the raccoon. "I need to find a cage for this little bandit. Cora, run upstairs and get my Polaroid camera. Stella—do you know where I keep the extra collars?"

"Bottom right drawer of your desk."

"Okay, grab all I've got."

Stella hurried into the office and picked up a handful of bright-yellow collars. They came in three different sizes. Stella took the collars into the boarder room, where Anya had just placed the raccoon in a wire cage.

"I got the camera," Cora announced as she joined them.

"You girls can put a yellow collar on any dog or cat that isn't wearing one," Anya said. "That will make the strays easy to pick out if anyone comes in looking for a missing pet."

"Cool," Stella said.

"Take a photo of the strays, too," Anya added. "We'll make some posters and put them up at the Red Cross shelter."

Stella nodded. She felt sorry for the people who had to stay at the shelter. People like Marisa and her mom. They didn't have much to do except hang out and wait. Wait to see when—if—they were allowed to go home. It sounded miserable. And it would be even worse if you were missing a pet.

"Let's start with the cats," Cora suggested.

"Okay." Stella followed her sister into Exam One.

Fourteen cages were filled with fourteen cats. The early arrivals had gotten the best accommodations—three-foot-square cages complete with cushions, litter boxes, and food and water bottles. But Anya only had six of these deluxe cages, and the later arrivals were in kitty carrying cases.

Stella and Cora slowly moved around the room.

Blue cards had been filled out for the cats that had been dropped off by their owners. Only two of the cats were missing cards.

"This one's a stray," Stella said. She opened the door of the cage—one of the smaller ones.

Cora reached in and lifted out an orange cat. The tom's face had started to go gray, and most of his teeth were missing. His fur was dusty with soot. His right paw was damp—he'd licked it and used it to clean his fur.

"Wait—he has a collar," Cora reported. "See if you can read it."

Stella picked up the small heart-shaped medal on the collar. "Fifi. There's a phone number."

"Write it down and I'll try to call," Cora said.

While her sister went to make the call, Stella put Fifi back in his cage. She continued around the room.

Only one other cat was missing a blue card.

Stella stopped next to the cage and peered inside. A small face stared out at her. The kitten was a mess—so much soot was worked into her coat that Stella couldn't tell what color her fur was.

"Mrrraaaaoooowww!"

The kitten really put herself into that meow. For several seconds, Stella had a perfect view of the kitten's rough white-pink tongue, her ridged hard palate, and all her tiny needlelike teeth.

"Hey—what's the problem?" Stella asked. "Are you hungry?" She knew small creatures needed to eat more often than big ones. That's why babies were always waking up in the middle of the night. Stella had learned that taking care of Rufus when he was tiny.

She unlatched the cage and lifted the little kitten out.

"Mrrraaaaaoooowww!"

Something about that meow. It was too intense. Too desperate to be just hunger. Stella held the kitten with one hand. She twisted the little thing around and carefully looked her over. The kitten spread out her stick legs for balance.

There! On the bottom of one paw. The fur was singed black. And the kitten's pad was bright red and blistered. It was a small burn—easy to miss, but painful-looking.

"Poor sweetie," Stella said, putting the kitten on her chest. The kitten hung on for dear life, sinking her thin claws into Stella's shirt.

Cora came back into the room. "I found Fifi's owner!" she said triumphantly. "She'd changed the message on her answering machine before she got evacuated. She's staying at her son's house in Billings. She really freaked when she heard I'd found her cat. Pure joy."

"That's great," Stella said. "Come help me with this kitten. She has a burned paw."

The girls carried the kitten into Exam Two. Stella and Cora took turns washing their hands and putting on a mask and gloves.

"You hold her and I'll rinse out the burn," Stella said. She filled a large dose syringe with the same fluid Anya had used on the raccoon. While Cora held the kitten's paw steady, Stella squeezed the liquid out.

"Mrrraaaaoooowwwmrrraaaaoooowww!" The kitten howled in protest and scrambled to get away.

"I think that hurts her!" Cora said.

"Is she scratching you?"

"No."

"Then let's keep going," Stella said. She tried not to let the kitten's protests make her hurry. Cleaning out the burn properly was too important to rush.

The kitten's howls went on and on. Stella felt queasy. She felt as if someone was poking her own toes with needles. A syringe full of saline. Another. And another.

"Shh, kitty, it's okay," Cora kept whispering.

Scissors. Gauze. Tape. Making the bandage so

it wouldn't bother the kitten was tricky. Especially since Stella's hands were shaking.

"Rrraaaaooo . . ." The kitten was starting to go hoarse.

"Done!" Stella said. She let out her breath.

"Finally," Cora said. "Can we give her some milk now?"

"Sure," Stella said. "I'll hold her while you get it."

Stella took the kitten from Cora, keeping her at arm's length. She expected the kitten to scratch her. To draw some blood for all the pain Stella had put her through. But the little cat just hung limply. Maybe she was too tired to fight.

"You think I'm a big meanie, don't you?" Stella asked the kitten. She pulled it closer, snuggling it against her chest. She petted the kitten's head and the kitten pushed up against her hand, closing her eyes with pleasure.

Stella leaned against the exam table. "I wonder what color you are under all that soot."

"I think she's white," Cora said as she came back into the room.

White . . . That made Stella think of Rufus. Poor Rufus. What was happening to him at that moment? It was after six. Past his dinnertime. Was he hungry? Or worse . . .

Stella was so wrapped up in her sad thoughts

that she didn't notice at first. The kitten had started to purr.

"Here's some milk," Cora said, placing a small bowl on the exam table. Stella put the kitten down and she immediately started lapping up the milk.

"What a sweetie," Cora said.

"Girls! The people from the Humane Society are here!" Anya was calling from the waiting room.

Stella and Cora quickly put the kitten in her cage. "Don't worry, Sooty," Stella said. "We'll be back soon."

Stella was excited. Help was finally here! Someone to rescue Rufus. She rushed into the waiting room.

Norma, Anya, and Jack were all there. Jack must have just gotten back from Papa Pete's. He was still holding his keys.

The three of them were talking to three elderly women—probably ladies who had lost their parakeets or poodles.

"Where are the animal rescuers?" Stella demanded.

Norma gave her a puzzled smile. "Right here. Bertha, Ida, Lillian—I'd like you to meet my daughters. Cora is the big one. Stella is the little one."

"Hi," Cora said. "Hey, Dad—how's Papa Pete?"

"Fine, fine," Jack said. "He says he's been through much worse."

All Stella could do was stare. She felt as if someone had sucked the air out of her lungs. She wasn't sure what she had expected, but it wasn't three . . . grannies.

These ladies had gray hair. One of them—Stella thought it was Ida—was wearing a *skirt*. How were they going to handle goats? And Dobermans?

She couldn't possibly trust these old women to save Rufus.

Bertha was coming toward Cora and Stella, holding out her wrinkly hand.

"Nice to meet you, girls," Bertha said, giving their hands a fast shake. "Now, we have only a few hours of daylight and a lot of work to do. So let's get cracking."

There's only one thing to do, Stella decided. "I want to come with you," she said. "I know the valley better than you do. And . . . And I'm also a lot younger."

Bertha smiled. "Thanks for offering. But we need you here at the clinic. Taking care of all these animals is going to be heaps of work. Do you have a map of the barricaded area?"

"Um—sure," Anya said. "Somewhere."

"I've got one in the truck," Jack said.

Things started to happen fast.

Jack dug an old road map out of his glove compartment. He used Anya's copier to enlarge the barricaded valley. When he got it big enough, he pinned the map up on the bulletin board in Anya's office.

Anya got out a box of pins with yellow heads.

Bertha worked through the stack of requests. Each one was marked with a yellow pin on the map. Some clusters appeared and Bertha started to organize the requests by location.

Stella watched silently as Bertha, Ida, and Lillian worked. The yellow pin for Rufus was the last one added. Stella wanted to tell the grannies to save Rufus first. But she felt funny about it. Everyone loved their pets. She couldn't ask for special treatment.

• 7 •

"**S**tella! Are you guys here?"

Bertha looked up from passing out rescue assignments. "Who's that?" she asked, sounding slightly annoyed.

"Sounds like Josie," Stella said quickly. "I'll find out what she wants."

Josie Russell was Stella's best friend. She lived on a ranch about ten minutes outside of town.

Stella found Josie standing in the waiting room. She was holding a wicker picnic basket. The same wicker picnic basket she'd used a few months earlier to bring an injured duck into the clinic. She looked hot and sweaty and tired—same as everyone else.

"You evacuated?" Josie demanded.

"Yeah."

"Everyone okay?"

"Rufus is still in the house."

Josie didn't say anything. They stood just looking at each other for a few minutes. Stella knew Josie understood how she felt. After all, Josie had helped Stella nurse Rufus back to health.

"What's in the basket?" Stella asked.

"A cat. We've been helping the Bangs get their cattle and horses moved to the fairgrounds. Clem found this cat hiding out in the hay in one of the horse trailers. No tags. We were going to take him home. But he keeps throwing up."

"Take him into Exam Two. I'll get Anya."

A few minutes later, they stood peering into the basket.

The cat was an enormous gray and white tom. He looked like a fighter. He had a scab on his nose and a chunk was missing out of one ear.

"Is he wild?" Stella asked, because the tom was a mess. His legs were covered in soot up to his shoulders and he had some oily-looking splotches on his back. Tar, maybe.

Anya shook her head. "Too docile."

Some of the woods around Gateway were home to bands of wildcats. The cats had been dumped in the woods by people who moved or who had decided a pet was too much work.

Many of the abandoned animals died. Those that survived, bred. And since female cats can give birth every four months, the bands grew quickly.

The wildcats make Stella sad. Lots of them were sick and half starved. Serious diseases like feline leukemia spread quickly through their population.

Sometimes Anya placed traps for the wildcats. She gave shots to the ones she caught and fixed them so that they couldn't have more babies. The wildcats were scared of people and very hard to catch. Most would never, ever let a person pick them up.

But the scratched-up tom seemed perfectly relaxed when Anya picked him up and put him on the exam table.

"Was he caught in the fire?" Josie asked.

"Hmm . . ." Anya squeezed the cat's mouth so that he opened his jaw. She examined his gums. "Well, there are no signs of smoke poisoning," she said.

Anya checked out the cat's paws. And his whiskers. "No burns, either. I think this old tom was just out hunting in a burned-out building. Or maybe in a part of the forest where the fire had already passed through. He's picked up an awful lot of ash."

"Is that bad?" Josie asked.

"Not too bad," Anya said. "Licking up the soot will make him sick, that's all. I'd suggest giving him a good bath and some decent food."

"I can do that," Josie said.

Anya gave Josie a smile. "Great. We're all out of beds in our cat ward at the moment."

Stella helped Josie get the tom back in his basket. As soon as her friend left, she followed Anya into her office. Anya was the only one in the room.

"What happened to Bertha, Ida, and Lillian?" Stella asked.

"They went out on their first run," Anya explained.

"Good," Stella said. "Anya, lots of the cats in Exam One are sooty, too. Do they need baths?"

"It would be a good idea," Anya said. "But right now I need to check the strays we've taken in. I want to make sure they're not carrying any diseases."

"Cora and I can take care of the cats," Stella said. "Where is Cora?"

"Walking dogs."

"When she gets back, ask her to come help me in Exam One."

"Will do."

Getting the cat bath organized didn't take long. Exam One had a deep slop sink in one corner. Stella put in the stopper and filled the sink about halfway. She found a bottle of pet shampoo and a bunch of old towels, and put them next to the sink.

Cora came in just as Stella was pulling a couple of pairs of heavy work gloves out of a drawer.

"This is crazy," Cora said. "It's like suddenly having a hundred pets. By the time we finish feeding and walking them it will be time to start all over again."

Stella grinned and tossed her sister a pair of gloves. "Pretty much my idea of a perfect life."

"So which one of the cats is going to be our first victim?" Cora asked.

"You pick."

Cora decided on Fifi—the cat whose owner she had tracked down.

Fifi was quiet as Cora lifted him out of his cage. But he began to struggle the minute Cora approached the water.

"Ouch!" Cora cried as he tried to scramble over her shoulder.

Stella grabbed the cat and quickly placed him in the sink. "Hold him down!" she told Cora.

Cora grabbed the tom's front legs in one hand and put her other hand on his back and pushed down. "Cool it, kitty," she said. "This is for your own good."

Stella turned on the water and pulled out the little spray nozzle that was attached to the sink. She aimed it at Fifi's back.

Total kitty panic.

"Hhhheeee," Fifi hissed. He arched his back and his tail stood up as straight as a flagpole. Ears back. Stella had the impression his fur

would have been puffed up—if it hadn't been slicked down by the water.

"Oh—this was a good idea," Cora groaned.

"I'll try to hurry." Stella grabbed the shampoo and squirted some into her hand. She rubbed it into Fifi's fur. The soap foam was a sooty gray color.

Fifi reached one paw toward the edge of the sink. He was trying to hook his claws over the rim, desperately scrambling to escape.

"Mrrrrrr . . ."

"Why do cats hate water so much?" Cora asked.

Stella was busy working the shampoo through Fifi's fur. "They're desert animals."

"Well, I think it's because they look pathetic wet," Cora said.

"That's not nice," Stella said.

She started rinsing Fifi with the spray. The poor cat did look pitiful—about half his normal size. Bony. He even gave up fighting. He just stood with a posture that clearly said: I'm miserable.

Stella finished with the water. She grabbed a towel.

"Can you hand him out?" she asked Cora.

"Okay." Cora lifted the dripping cat and handed him to Stella. Stella grabbed him. And then . . .

"Hhhhheeee!" Fifi reached out and slashed at Stella's nose.

"Ahh!" Stella leaned back and dropped the cat. Fifi ran under the exam table and shook himself indignantly.

"Did he get you?" Cora asked.

"Just missed."

Stella took a couple of deep breaths, and then started to laugh. "Man, that is one irritated kitty."

"Irritated but clean."

Stella picked up the towel and started to let the dirty water out of the sink. "Next time, I'll hold on better."

Cora put Fifi's cage on the floor and filled his bowl with some stinky wet food. Fifi—keeping low to the ground and watching them warily—slunk back inside. His fur was sticking out in all directions.

When the water was deep enough, Stella went and got the kitten with the burned paw out of her cage. She gently removed the bandage.

"Okay, get ready for war," Cora said. "This time I'll do the shampoo."

"Okay." Stella slowly lowered the kitten into the water.

"Rwoow?"

"It's okay," Stella crooned.

The kitten's little body went stiff. She was shaking—probably with fear, since the water was warm. But she didn't hiss or extend her claws.

Cora worked quickly, rubbing lather into the kitten's fur and rinsing it off.

"Look," Stella said as she lifted her out of the water. "She's all white."

"Maybe because she's such an angel," Cora said as she wrapped the towel around the kitten and gently dried her off.

"I wonder who she belongs to," Stella said, running her finger down the kitten's nose.

"I think her tags got yanked off somehow," Cora said. "She couldn't be a stray."

"I hope she gets to go home soon," Stella said. But that was only partly true. Another part of Stella was hoping that Sooty wouldn't be claimed, and that she'd be able to take the sweet kitten home.

If she ever got to go home.

• 8 •

"Cora! Stella!" Norma cried. "Bertha is back. Come help unload her van."

For a moment, Stella couldn't breathe. Then her heart started thumping wildly. She couldn't get to the van fast enough. And yet she was afraid to go. She was hoping to see Rufus in one of Bertha's cages.

Cora grabbed Stella's arm. "Come on!"

They ran outside.

Bertha had backed her van right up over the sidewalk and onto the patch of grass in front of the clinic. She was a worse driver than Anya.

The doors of the van were open. Anya and Norma and Jack stood waiting to help unload the animals.

Please let Rufus be in there, Stella thought.

"You guys are never going to believe this one,"

Bertha said. She sounded amused, which bugged Stella a bit. It seemed rude for Bertha to be enjoying herself when their house might be burning down.

Bertha swung open the back doors of the van. She reached in and pulled a dog carrier toward her.

Stella peered around Cora's shoulder and looked inside. She could see a furry form squooshed way up against the back of the carrier.

"I was heading to the cabin with the pair of Dobermans," Bertha said. She had one foot up in the van. "Wasn't expecting to find much since the place was back in the woods. When I got there, the cabin didn't look too good. But the dog run was out in the open. Dogs seemed fine, although they sure didn't want anything to do with me."

Sugar and Honey, Stella thought. She was glad they were safe.

"I finally lured them out with some water," Bertha said. "Took a good twenty minutes. And the whole time I kept hearing this . . . sound I couldn't identify. It sounded a little bit like my husband snoring. When he has a cold. Couldn't for the life of me figure out what it was."

"What did you do?" Stella asked.

"First I got those two 'fraidy cats loaded into the van. Then I went to investigate. Farther back in the woods, I found a detached garage. The fire had missed it. Which was lucky because something definitely was alive in there. The snoring sound was louder."

Anya shifted her weight, clearly impatient for Bertha to get to the point.

But Bertha was enjoying her story. She didn't seem to think there was any reason to hurry. "I yelled 'Hello!' And the entire garage—it didn't look too sturdy—started to shake."

Stella shot a look at Cora.

"I approached carefully," Bertha continued. "I was expecting to find a large dog. Maybe a German shepherd or a wolfhound. Only, of course, I'd never heard an animal make a sound like the one I was hearing."

"What did you find?" Norma asked. She sounded more concerned than curious.

"See for yourself." Bertha stepped aside so that they could peer into the carrier.

Cora and Stella stepped closer. Small round ears. A tan snout. Thick brown fur. And a plump body.

"It's a bear cub!" Stella exclaimed.

Norma hurried forward. "You're joking!"

Stella moved aside so that her mother could get a good look.

"You're not joking," Norma said. "It's a brown bear. About five months old."

"How'd you get him in the case?" Anya asked Bertha.

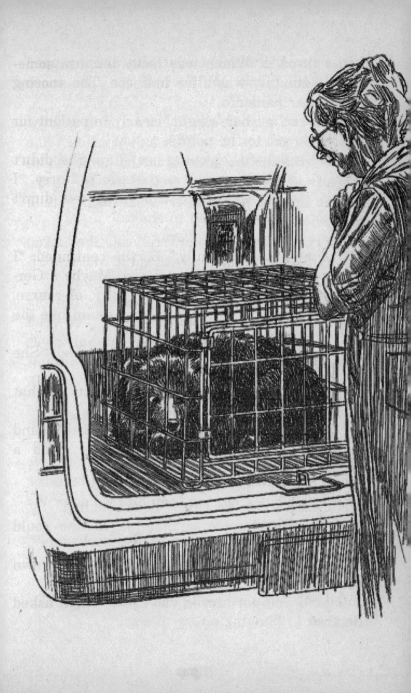

"Just threw a blanket over him and wrapped him up. He didn't put up half the fuss those ninny Dobermans did."

"That's not a good sign," Norma said grimly. "I'd better call this in to Fish and Wildlife." She asked Bertha for the address of the home where the bear had been kept and trotted into the clinic.

"What are we going to do with him?" Stella asked Anya.

Anya ran a hand over her forehead. She looked tired, and Stella suddenly realized it was late afternoon. They had been going hard all day.

"I have no idea," Anya said wearily. "Raising bears for release is specialized stuff. I've read about facilities where they have special cages that allow the handlers to feed the bears without ever coming into contact with them. They watch the bears through video cameras."

"Is this bear really wild?" Jack asked. "Someone has been keeping him in a garage."

"True . . . ," Anya said with a sigh. "I guess we can call some facilities. Maybe they can take the bear in. But where can we keep him for now? We have a full house."

"Couldn't we build a cage in the back yard?" Stella asked.

"We've got about fifteen dogs back there," Anya pointed out. "And we really don't want to get this bear used to hanging out with dogs."

Everyone was quiet for a moment.

"What if . . . what if we got rid of the dogs somehow?" Stella asked.

"How?" Cora demanded.

"We could move them somewhere," Stella said.

"In case you forgot, our house is slightly inaccessible!" Cora shouted.

"I didn't forget! I was thinking of someone like Marisa. . . ."

"Marisa and her mom are at the shelter."

"I know."

"Girls . . . ," Jack said.

"They don't allow animals at the shelter."

"Cora! I know! I'm just thinking out loud!" An image of Marisa and her mom popped into Stella's mind. They were hanging out in the high school gym. And their animals were outside, pressing their noses against the windows and whining to get in.

Bingo!

"Anya," Stella said. "Couldn't we set up a temporary dog run at the high school? Somewhere outside? Separate from the main building so that the Red Cross wouldn't mind?"

"I bet the lumberyard would donate some poles and wire," Jack said. "It would be great publicity."

Norma came trotting back down the back steps. "Looks like we're going to have to hang onto that little guy for a while. Fish and Wildlife personnel have been reassigned to other duties during the fire."

"Try the lumberyard," Anya told Jack.

"Come on, Cora," Jack said. "I might need help."

"Norma, why don't you come with me?" Anya suggested. "We need to talk the Red Cross into opening a dog run on their property."

"It's not their property," Stella pointed out.

"Right," Anya said. "So maybe we'll talk to the school principal."

"What's going on?" Norma demanded.

Anya explained their plan.

It took a couple of hours to arrange. By the time Norma and Anya got the Red Cross and Board of Education people to agree, Jack and Cora had arrived with the materials to build the pen. Half a dozen people who were sitting around in the shelter came out to put it together.

Marisa, Cora, and Stella went back to the clinic for the dogs. There were seventeen of them, now that Honey and Sugar had been unloaded.

"This is great, just great," Marisa kept saying. And Stella could tell she meant it. Marisa was happy to have something to do.

Something other than imagining her house burning down.

Something other than worrying about her horses and pigs.

Stella realized how lucky she was to have been busy all day. Busy meant no time to think.

Cora and Stella handed the dogs over to Marisa and her mom. Then they hurried back to the clinic. Lillian and Ida had brought in another batch of rescued animals while they were gone.

Stella kept thinking about Rufus. They *must* have gotten Rufus this time.

"Hey, girls," Jack greeted them. "I'm glad you're here. We've got two more dogs that need to be walked over to the shelter."

"Did they . . . go to our house?" Stella asked.

"Sorry, Muffin."

Back to the shelter. Back to the clinic.

By that time, Anya and Norma had moved the dog carrier with the bear into Anya's dog run.

"What's happening?" Stella called.

"Shhh . . . , " Norma said.

Stella fell silent, guessing that her mother didn't want the bear to get used to hearing human voices. She watched as Norma used a pole syringe to inject the bear. *Something to put him to sleep,* Stella thought.

Most anesthetics took about ten minutes to take effect.

Waiting.

Waiting.

Waiting.

Under the smoky haze, the sky above the clinic

seemed to be a deep blue. Only a few hours of daylight were left.

Normally Stella would take Rufus outside to work on his obedience training around this time. He was finally mastering the sit. In another week or two, he'd have it.

Stella's throat suddenly felt thick with unshed tears. Rufus may never learn to sit now. . . .

Something was happening.

Norma was opening the carrier. She knelt down and pulled out the limp cub. She had to use two arms. The cub was about the size of a four-month-old Labrador, but he was much more solidly built.

Cora, Stella, and Norma followed Anya inside. She carried the cub into Exam Two and put him on the scale.

"Twenty-two pounds," Anya said. She got out a pad of paper and started taking notes.

"Is that good?" Stella asked.

"I'm not sure," Anya admitted. "But my guess is no."

She ran her hand over the sleeping bear's side. "I can feel his ribs. I don't think this little guy has had a solid meal in weeks."

"Fur is pretty mangy," Norma said, pulling on a pair of gloves.

Stella felt anger boiling up inside her. "I just don't understand some people. First they kidnap a bear. And then they don't even feed him!"

"Not so fast," Norma said. "I'd say whoever has been keeping this bear probably found him in pretty rough shape. He is almost certainly an orphan. Mama bears don't let people snatch their babies."

Stella felt a little bit ashamed. Whoever had hauled this cub out of the woods was probably trying to save it. "Well, they could have at least fed him," she said sullenly.

"Probably tried," Anya said. "But whoever has been keeping this bear probably found him up a tree and weak with hunger."

"Then they were scared to ask for advice," Norma said. "After all, having a brown bear cub in your backyard is sort of . . . against the law."

"Can you save him?"

Anya nodded. "I don't see why not. Some fluids. Lots of berries, milk, and fish. We'll get him fattened up before he goes off to the rescue facility."

"This is one animal the fire may have saved," Norma said.

Stella looked out the window. The light was starting to fade from the sky.

• 9 •

Brring! Brring!

"Could you get the phone, Stella?" Anya asked. "My hands are full."

Stella grinned as she dashed out into the hallway. Anya's hands were full, all right. Full of twenty-two pounds of brown bear.

"Hello? Goodwin Animal Clinic."

"Stella? Is that you? It's Marisa. I'm calling on my mom's cell phone and the batteries aren't too good."

Stella's stomach gave one of those bad-news lurches. Even through the cell-phone static, she could tell that Marisa sounded frantic. "What's the matter? Did you hear something about Clemmy?" Stella knew how worried Marisa was about her pig.

"No," Marisa said breathlessly. "But you'd better get over here. Two of the dogs you dropped off are fighting."

Fighting? That didn't make sense. "You didn't take their muzzles off, did you?" Stella demanded.

"Well, sure. Those things are cruel. The dogs can't even open their mouths."

"That's the idea," Stella snapped. "Listen, we'll be right over."

"Hurry!" Marisa said.

Stella trotted back into Exam Two. "Dogfight," she announced. "At the Red Cross shelter. Marisa and her mom don't know what to do."

Anya looked at Norma. "I'll go. Bears are more your specialty than mine."

Norma nodded. "Be careful."

"I will," Anya said.

They sounded tense—which seemed a bit odd to Stella. She expected to see some bloodied dogs when they got to the shelter. Not pleasant. But not anything that Anya didn't see every week.

"Do you want me to come?" Stella offered.

"Sure."

Stella and Anya ran out to the 4x4. It had only been about twenty minutes since Stella was last outside. But the smoke seemed more dense. Stella's eyes immediately started to sting.

Anya's eyes were watering.

"Can you see to drive?" Stella asked.

"No choice."

Anya cranked up her window, so Stella did the same. The 4x4 didn't have any air-conditioning and it immediately got hot inside. Anya turned up the fan.

"Look in the glove compartment," Anya said as she pulled onto the road. "See if you can find bandanas. Wet them down with water from the cooler."

Stella found a blue bandanna. Then a yellow one that had something spilled on it. Coffee. Or maybe blood. She tried not to think about it as she wet them down.

"Now what?" she asked Anya.

"Tie one around your nose and mouth. Give the other one to me."

Stella hesitated for a moment. Then she handed Anya the blue bandana, and tied the stained one around her nose.

Stain? What stain? Stella could suddenly breathe much better. Not normally, but better.

The first thing Stella could see when Anya pulled into the parking lot was a crowd around the dog run. Marisa and her mother were there.

Stella couldn't see the dogs yet. But she steeled herself for an awful sight.

They hopped out of the truck.

"Errrr . . ."

"Ruffruffruffruff!"

"They're still fighting!" Stella exclaimed.

Anya shot her a surprised look. "What did you expect? They usually don't stop until you pull them apart or one of them's dead."

"Coming through!" Anya shouted. The crowd recognized her and parted.

Stella hesitated. So they weren't here to patch up a couple of bad-mannered dogs. They were here to break up a fight. But dogs had big teeth. And strong jaws. And these two sounded pretty angry.

"Errrrerrrerrrr . . ." The growl was deep and menacing.

"Ruffruffruff—yipyip!" A sudden cry of pain.

Stella got up her nerve and pushed through the crowd. To her surprise, she immediately recognized one of the dogs. Amber. A Welsh corgi. Stella had popped a ball out of his throat a few months earlier.

Corgis aren't exactly huge.

And the other dog was even smaller. Some sort of cattle dog mix. Nothing more than a pup.

Two little dogs fighting. . . . The scene would have been almost funny if they hadn't been yelping and barking and growling so fiercely.

The pup was bleeding from one ear. And Amber kept nipping at him. Going for his feet.

Then his neck. Trying to find a place to sink his teeth in.

Mrs. Capra came up beside Stella. "Stop them," she pleaded.

Anya blew out her breath. "Getting between two angry dogs is dangerous. I'm going to need someone's help."

"I'll help," Mrs. Capra said. "Just tell me what to do."

Anya considered for a moment, and then shook her head. "Sorry, Belle. But I think you're a bit too upset. Stella, can you do exactly what I tell you to?"

"Um—sure." Stella was nervous and proud all at the same time. Anya needed someone she could trust to help her. And she'd picked Stella— even though they were surrounded by a crowd of adults.

Stella ignored the way her stomach was twisting. "What should I do?" she said, trying to sound eager.

"We're going to have to pull the dogs apart," Anya said. "You take the puppy—he seems less aggressive. I'll take Amber."

"Okay."

"Walk up behind the puppy and pick up his hind legs like you were picking up a wheelbarrow," Anya said calmly. "Then start to back up. The puppy will have to concentrate on not losing his balance and he'll forget the fight. Move in an S pattern so that the puppy can't turn around and bite you."

Stella giggled nervously. "No problem."

"You scared?"

"Yes."

"That's okay. Just pay attention to what you're doing."

Stella nodded.

"Ready?"

"Well . . . sure."

Anya unlatched the gate and walked into the dog run.

Stella followed her.

They got into position. Stella glanced at the crowd. She saw Marisa. She looked plenty worried.

"One, two, three . . . GO!" Anya counted.

Stella reached down and grabbed the puppy's furry brown feet. Quickly, in one fluid motion, she lifted them up ninety degrees.

Anya did the same thing to Amber.

"Arf?" The puppy twisted around and tried to see what was happening.

"Back up!" Anya called.

Oh. Right. Stella started to walk backward. Not too fast because the dog run wasn't very big. A little to the right, then a little to the left.

The puppy scrambled backward, struggling to walk on two feet.

Amber was doing the same thing. Only Anya was working her way toward the gate. "Open the gate," she called.

Someone opened the gate.

Anya pulled Amber right through.

Someone closed the gate.

Someone else grabbed Amber.

The crowd burst into applause.

Stella gently put the puppy's legs back on the ground. He immediately sat down and began to whine. Five minutes later, Anya was putting antibiotic ointment on his ear.

Mrs. Capra was putting muzzles back on all the dogs.

Marisa approached Stella. "Thanks."

"Sure."

Marisa was grinning.

Stella found herself smiling, too. She wasn't even sure why. "What's up?"

"Clemmy and her piglets are safe!" Marisa said.

"How?" Stella demanded.

"Some of the local ranchers are moving large animals. They evacuated Clemmy and the piglets to the fairgrounds. Our horses, too!"

Stella gave Marisa a hug. "That's great!" she said.

Maybe things were looking up.

Maybe Rufus would be waiting for Stella back at the clinic.

Anya came up to them. "I think I'm all done here. Marisa, just promise me you'll leave the muzzles on."

Marisa crossed her heart. "Promise."

"Ready to go, Stella?"

"Ready."

• 10 •

Stella didn't say much on the way back to the clinic. She felt like she'd been keeping her emotions tamped down all day. She kept telling herself if she waited another hour she'd see Rufus. And then another. And another.

She'd pushed the deadline back and back and back.

And now it was dark.

The day was over.

She couldn't wait anymore.

Anya pulled up in front of the clinic. Both of the Humane Society vans were parked in front. One of the grannies had to have saved Rufus. He must be inside.

"I want to check on the bear," Anya said.

Stella rushed inside. The clinic was quiet. The lights were turned off. Faint noises came from Anya's apartment. Pots and pans. Voices.

"Mom?" Stella called. She ran up the stairs.

"Shhh . . . ," Jack said. He pointed toward the living room. Cora was sitting in a chair in front of the TV. Her head was tilted to one side. She was fast asleep.

Norma was standing in front of Anya's little stove, flipping grilled cheese sandwiches. A box of frozen peas sat on the counter.

"Where are the grannies?" Stella demanded.

"They went to the shelter to sleep," Norma said quietly. "We tried to convince them to stay here, but they wouldn't hear of it."

"They're going to sleep?" Stella was breathless with disappointment.

"Muffin, they're only human," Jack said. "Besides, it's dark. Going out now is too dangerous for them. For anyone."

"It's been a long day," Norma said.

Stella agreed. She was so tired she felt as if she could close her eyes and fall asleep standing up. But so what?

"Rufus has been alone all day!" Stella burst out. "He hasn't had any water. He hasn't had any food. He has to be thirsty and scared and . . . how can you think about going to sleep? There is no way we can leave him alone all night!"

"Muffin, what do you expect us to do?" Norma asked.

"Get in the truck, drive home, and get Rufus!"

Norma and Jack exchanged uh-oh looks.

Cora stirred and sat up. She was awake now. Nobody said anything.

"Fine!" Stella stormed. "Sit here and eat grilled cheese. I'm going home!"

She turned and moved toward the stairs. *Where is my bike?* she wondered. She hadn't seen it since that morning.

Jack reached out and grabbed Stella's arm. "Whoa. Hang on a minute. Have a seat. Let's talk."

Stella was breathing hard with anger. But she let her father pull her back toward the couch. She flopped down and crossed her arms over her chest.

Jack and Norma sat down, facing Stella.

"I know you've been thinking about Rufus all day," Norma said.

"I think we all have," Jack said.

Stella could see Cora nod.

"You know that we all love Rufus," Norma said. "But our own safety is more important."

Stella wanted to argue. But then she thought of the stable. She remembered the angry, frightened look on Anya's face.

But this was different, wasn't it? She wasn't suggesting going into a burning building. Just driving to their house and only going in if it *wasn't* burning.

"Couldn't we just go check it out?" Stella asked. "If it looks too dangerous, we could turn around."

"Muffin, what if we went into the valley and something happened to us? What would happen if a burning tree fell on the road and we couldn't get around it?"

"We could take the phone out and call for help," Stella said.

"Exactly," Norma said. "And someone would have to come save us. Sheriff Rose, maybe. And then what if she got hurt?"

"It would be my fault," Stella said sullenly.

"It's hard," Jack said. "But waiting is really the best thing we can do. The *only* thing."

Norma put her hand on Stella's knee and gave her a little squeeze. "Do you want mustard on your grilled cheese?"

"No."

Jack and Norma went back into the kitchen.

Cora picked up the remote. She changed stations. The news. Pictures of the fire. Cora groaned and clicked off the set. She closed her eyes and stretched out on the couch.

Stella closed her eyes, too. But she couldn't sleep. She couldn't get the image of Rufus out of her mind. The worst part was thinking that he was afraid.

The living room door opened. *Must be Anya,* Stella thought.

Stella heard Cora gasp. She opened her eyes. The swimming pool raccoon was walking across the carpet. Lumbering, like a miniature bear. Relaxed, like he owned the place.

"Mom!" Stella hissed, without taking her eyes off the raccoon. He moved over to the coffee table, sat back on his hind legs, and surveyed the magazines on top.

Stella heard footsteps, and then her mother gasped. "Who let him out of his cage?" Norma whispered.

"Not me," Stella said.

They watched as the raccoon picked up the remote and turned it around so that it was facing the TV.

"I think . . . he let himself out," Cora said. "His paws are . . . like, totally *hands*."

The raccoon nosed at the couch, and then climbed up. Cora scooted out of the way as the raccoon sat back against the cushions, exposing his belly, and turned on the TV.

"No way," Jack whispered. Stella wasn't sure when he had come in.

The news was still on. Weather. Tomorrow was going to be hot and dry.

Click. Click. The raccoon used his tiny "thumb" to change channels. He finally settled on a nature program.

More footsteps. Anya came in and did a massive double take. "Guys? You really should ask before you invite guests over."

Jack started to laugh. Quietly at first. And then louder.

Stella smiled and then laughed herself.

The raccoon was not amused. He got down off the couch and moved closer to the TV. Like he was having a hard time hearing.

That just made the whole situation funnier. Pretty soon, tears were rolling down Stella's cheeks.

Norma was the first one to sober up. "Come on, guys. Dinner is getting cold."

"What do we do about the raccoon?" Stella asked.

"Try luring him back downstairs with a piece of bread," Anya said. "Or, better yet, a couple of peanuts."

"I'll do it!" Stella found the peanuts in the cupboard. She grabbed a handful and held one out to the raccoon.

Instant interest. The raccoon snatched the peanut, unshelled it, popped it in his mouth, and held out his paw for more.

"You like that, huh? Well, if you want more, you're going to have to come downstairs." Stella held out another peanut and began backing toward the stairs.

The raccoon hopped off the couch and lolled after her. She gave him two more peanuts on the steps, another in the back hallway, and dumped the rest into the food bowl in his cage.

As soon as the raccoon crawled inside, Stella closed and latched the door. But wouldn't he just let himself out again? She looked for something to secure the latch. Finally she got a rubber band and wrapped it around the latch several times. The raccoon shouldn't be able to reach that from inside.

Stella checked on the raccoon again after dinner. He was curled up in the hollow log Anya had placed inside his cage, fast asleep.

She moved around the boarder room and Exam

One, making sure all of the animals had water. Fifi was sleeping with his head on his two front paws. He looked much better clean.

Stella peeked in at Sooty.

The kitten saw her. She stood up, stretched, and yawned. She put one tiny white paw on the wire of her cage. "Mmmww."

"Hi, sweetie," Stella said. She unlatched the cage and lifted the little kitten out.

Sooty snuggled close, shut her eyes, and broke into a loud purr.

Stella walked back to the boarder room and laid down on the cot there. She put Sooty on her chest, and petted her.

A little while later, Norma came downstairs. She sat on the edge of the cot. "You okay down here?"

"I guess."

Norma smoothed back the fur on Sooty's head. "What a pretty kitten."

"She's a stray."

"If nobody claims her, maybe you can keep her."

Stella didn't answer.

After a few minutes, Norma whispered good night, gave Stella a kiss on the forehead, and went back upstairs.

Stella stared at the ceiling. She knew what was behind her mom's offer. Norma thought that

Rufus might be . . . might be dead. So she was offering this kitten as a replacement.

That's stupid, Stella thought. *I could never love another animal the way I love Rufus. Not even Sooty.*

Stella was sure she would never fall asleep. But suddenly she felt herself jarred awake.

"What?" She sat up, her heart beating double time. Something was wrong.

Sooty jumped off the cot.

Sirens! Loud sirens. They were close.

Stella jumped up, kicking off the covers someone had put on her. She had to wake everyone up! But where were they? She stopped for a moment, adrenaline rushing through her body.

Oh, right. Upstairs.

Stella scooped up Sooty, and plopped her back in her cage. Then she ran for the stairs. She was barefoot. Someone had taken off her shoes. How long had she been asleep?

Someone was pounding at the back door.

Stella threw it open. A fireman was standing on the porch. He was suited up in yellow gear. Behind him, Stella could see people scurrying around on the dark street.

Actually . . . the street wasn't totally dark. There was a strange sort of half-light. Stella had a creepy feeling it was coming from the fire.

"Are you here alone?" the fireman demanded.

"No, my family is upstairs."

"Wake them up immediately."

"Why? What's the matter?"

"The wind direction changed. The fire is heading toward town."

"What time is it?"

"Around two."

"Do we have to evacuate?"

"Not yet. But get ready." The fireman had already turned and headed down the stairs.

Get ready . . . get two dozen cats, a raccoon, several bunnies, a turtle, three parakeets, a brown bear cub and who knew what else *ready*? Sure, no problem.

"Mom? Dad?" Stella hollered. "We've got a problem!"

Jack was the first one downstairs. He came pounding down in sweats and hiking boots, and headed for the back door.

"Where are you going?"

"Up on the roof. Come on, you can help."

Stella pulled on her boots and hurried outside. By then, her father had put a metal ladder against the side of the building. He was climbing up, dragging the garden hose behind him.

"What are you doing?" Stella called.

"Wetting down the shingles." Jack reached the top of the ladder and clambered onto the roof.

"Why?"

"So a spark doesn't start the building burning."

"Oh." Stella didn't like that idea. Not at all. It suddenly hit her. The town could burn down. No more Gateway. No more animal clinic. Poof!

"Okay—I'm ready," Jack called. "Turn on the water."

Stella ran and did what her father asked. She turned on the water as high as it would go.

• 11 •

"**S**tella—wake up. Come on. I need some help."

Stella opened her eyes and sat up, feeling completely lost. She had no memory of going to sleep. Couldn't remember lying down. *Where am I?* she wondered.

A cot, cages, a tile floor—the boarder room at the clinic. The clinic . . . it was still there!

"Cora—what happened?"

"The wind shifted again. Away from town this time."

Stella pulled herself up and shook her legs to get the blood flowing again. It was light out. The grass was dewy. Morning. Hooray!

"What are you doing?"

"Well, we've got a lot of cats to feed. Not to mention a major amount of litter to clean."

"I'll do the litter."

Cora raised her eyebrows. "Cool."

"Where's Anya?"

"Delivering some dog food to the shelter."

"Where are Mom and Dad?"

"They walked down to the sheriff's station."

"How come?"

"There was this rumor earlier . . . they're letting some people back in the valley."

"You're kidding!"

"It's just a rumor," Cora said sternly. "Nobody knows anything about our house yet. Don't get your hopes up."

"Okay!" Stella felt like dancing. This was the first good news they'd had. Maybe, soon, she'd be able to rescue Rufus herself.

"Hey—where are the grannies?"

"They already left."

More good news! Maybe, if Stella couldn't rescue Rufus herself, the grannies would!

"Stella?" Jared Frye came around the corner of the building. "I heard you guys have a bear cub back here."

Stella had met Jared in school the year before. He liked animals almost as much as she did.

"Hi, Jared! Are you okay? You didn't get evacuated?"

"Nope. But the fireman came by and ordered my dad to clean out the yard. All the old leaves are a fire hazard. So where's the bear?"

"You can't see him," Stella said. "He's not allowed near humans."

Jared's face fell.

"We've got about a thousand other animals inside. Want to help me feed them?"

"Sure."

They wandered into the boarder room, and the raccoon immediately started making a loud noise.

"Hey!" Jared said. "It's Einstein! How'd he get here?"

"My mom found him out on Potters Road in someone's swimming pool."

"Is he okay?"

"Sure. We just gave him some oxygen and treated a burn. You know this raccoon?"

Jared looked a bit embarrassed. "Dad and I have been feeding him. We even taught him how to open the screen door."

"Does he watch TV with you?"

"Yeah! I've been trying to teach him how to use the remote control."

Stella laughed. "Well, you're a pretty good teacher!"

The raccoon continued making a racket. He sounded like a cross between a bird and an insect. He was making loads of eye contact with Jared.

"Can't we let him out?"

"I don't think Anya would like that."

"Hey, kids." Anya poked her head into the boarder room. "Did you get some breakfast, Stella?"

"Not yet. I was feeding the animals first."

"Anya," Jared said. "Can I take Einstein home? He doesn't look too happy in his cage."

"Einstein?"

Jared explained how he knew the raccoon.

Anya stood, shaking her head. "I have one word for you, young man. Zoonotic."

"Excuse me?"

"Diseases that humans can get from animals," Stella explained.

Anya dragged Jared into her office and gave him a book about rabies to read. But she also agreed to let him release Einstein in the woods behind his house.

Stella found an empty dog carrier, and gave Jared some peanuts to lure Einstein inside.

By then, she was starving, so she took a break to eat.

Cora came upstairs for a drink of water. "Exam One is getting pretty stinky."

"Okay. I'll do the litter boxes now."

Stella decided to start with Sooty's cage. She lifted the kitten out and put her on the exam table. Sooty sat down, tucked her tail around her feet, and started licking her good paw.

After several licks, she used her paw to clean
her ear.

"We're going to have to get a new name for
you," Stella told the kitten. "You're not sooty anymore." Now that the kitten was cleaned up, she
was pure white except for a tiny patch of black
inside her ear.

Inside?

Stella moved closer and bent back the kitten's ear. She peered inside. The black mark was actually two letters and a number: GW6. It looked as if someone had written it by hand with a magic marker. It was a tattoo.

Suddenly Stella didn't feel quite so happy.

Sooty wasn't a stray. Someone had tattooed this mark on her. All Stella had to do was make a single phone call, and Animal Control would contact her owner.

Stella almost wanted to pretend she never saw the tattoo. But what was the point? Sooner or later, her mom or Anya would notice it. Anya always checked strays for tattoos and microchips. These methods of marking pets were becoming more common. She'd be sure to examine Sooty as soon as things calmed down.

The litter boxes would have to wait. Stella wanted to make the call while she had the nerve. She hurried into Anya's office and found the Animal Control number on the bulletin board.

"Animal Control."

"Oh, hi. Um . . . I found a kitten with a tattoo."

"Thank you for calling. Give me the number and I'll contact the owner immediately."

"GW6."

Stella could hear a computer keyboard clicking.

"Hmm . . . the owner lives near Goldenrock. They're having a big forest fire out that way. Could be a while before we reach the kitty's owner."

"That's okay," Stella said immediately. "The kitten is safe here and we'll keep her as long as necessary."

Stella gave the operator the name and address of the clinic. Then she hung up the phone and slumped down in Anya's office chair. Her good mood was completely gone. Sure, she *might* see Rufus again soon. But, then again, the fire could have burned down her house. And now Sooty was going away, too. Maybe not right away. But she was going.

The phone rang.

Stella stared at it for a moment. Something told her that was Sooty's family, calling to say they were coming to get her. She didn't want to answer the phone.

Brring!

"Goodwin Animal Clinic."

"Stella, is that you?" It was Sheriff Rose.

Something in her voice made Stella stand up. "Yes?"

"I'm out on Route 2A. Tell your aunt to get here immediately. A barn just collapsed."

"Route 2A—isn't that behind the barricade?"

"Not anymore. The owners just had time to

move their livestock back in before the whole thing gave way on them."

"How many animals?"

"Don't know. Cows, goats, a pig—at least one. Come quick!"

• 12 •

Stella rode out to Route 2A with Anya.

They brought all sorts of equipment. Anya wanted to be prepared no matter what they found.

Things didn't look good from the road. One side of a big red barn had completely given way.

"Why would a barn collapse now?" Stella wondered as they barreled down the driveway. "Don't we have enough problems?"

"They probably decided the barn was safe without realizing that the fire had weakened the structure."

"Wouldn't they see some fire damage?"

Anya yawned broadly. "Maybe they were too tired to look." She pulled to a stop behind Sheriff Rose's cruiser, took a deep breath, and slowly climbed out. Stella was right behind her.

Sheriff Rose came out to meet them. She

looked a bit sheepish, as well as completely exhausted. Her usually tidy hair was falling out of its braid.

"Rose," Anya said. "What do we have?"

Rose rubbed her hand over her face. "It's not as bad as I thought. The cattle got out okay. And the pigs were in the part of the barn that didn't collapse."

Anya relaxed slightly. "So none of the animals are injured?"

"Well, we've got a pinned goat."

"Pinned by what?" Anya asked in an I-don't-like-the-sound-of-this voice.

"A roof beam."

Anya grabbed a bag out of the back and headed toward the barn at a jog.

"Wait outside," Anya told Stella.

"But . . ."

"Just wait."

So Stella stood in the gravel driveway, peering into the barn.

Anya and Rose went inside.

Stella could see them—plus the backs of two adults and a couple of little kids. Just from the way they were standing, Stella could tell they were tired.

It was hard to see in the half-light of the barn, but Stella thought she could make out a beam. It was one of those enormous old wooden beams you see in ceilings sometimes. The beam lay across the short side of the barn. It had smashed through the walls enclosing a couple of stalls.

Stella could also hear the goat bleating desperately. Such a sad sound.

"Hello, I'm Anya Goodwin. I don't believe we've met." The adults conferred for several minutes. Stella saw them get into position and try to lift the beam. It didn't budge.

Suddenly everyone was heading outside. The family gave Stella a quick smile and hustled toward the house. The children were clinging to their mother's legs—shy, or maybe upset about seeing their goat trapped.

"What's happening?" Stella demanded.

"Gif is going to call some of his neighbors to help move the beam," Anya said. "I'm going to give the goat a sedative to calm him down."

Stella nodded. "Can I come in?"

"Yeah. It looks safe enough."

Stella took a deep breath and walked into the barn. The goat was still bleating. He sounded awful. Like he was in pain.

"It's okay, baby," Stella whispered. Slowly— frightened of what she would see—she crept closer.

Okay. It wasn't too bad. The goat's head and

body were mostly free. Stella couldn't see much blood—and nothing nastier.

The goat lifted up his head to look at her. "Blllaaahhh," he bleated.

Stella knelt down next to his head and gently petted his cheek. "It's okay," she murmured. "We're going to get you out of here."

Anya came in and injected the goat in his neck.

Stella sat down. For the next twenty minutes, she stroked the goat's head as a group of people began gathering in the yard. Two people. Then six. Then twenty.

"Okay, make some room," the farmer finally said.

Stella scrambled to her feet as all the people positioned themselves on either side of the beam. She slipped her fingers under the beam not far from the goat.

"On the count of three," Gif called. "One, two, three—*lift!*"

Stella lifted, but she could tell she wasn't doing much of the work.

Anya scrambled around and lifted the goat out of danger. She carried him outside and put him down on a blanket she had waiting.

Stella hurried out after her aunt. "How is he?"

Anya was frowning. "Worse than I thought."

"Is his leg broken?"

"Yes, but that's not what I'm worried about. He's got a bad splinter in his cheek. I'm afraid it might have punctured his eye."

Crash! BOOM!

Gif and his neighbors had let go of the beam.

"Can't you pull it out?" Stella asked.

"I'm not sure that's a good idea," Anya said. "That may just injure the eye further. I'd rather take an X ray first."

Anya sounded gloomy.

Stella thought she knew why. X rays and surgery were expensive. Most people wouldn't spend hundreds of dollars fixing up an injured goat when they could buy a new one for less.

"How's he look?" The farmer came out and wiped his hands on his already dusty overalls. The man's wife came out and stood beside him. The kids were still in the house—probably sleeping.

"Not good," Anya admitted. "I think his eye could be in danger. Plus, we've got a nasty break."

The couple exchanged weary looks. Deciding whether the goat was worth the cash. Stella steeled herself.

"It's been a rough couple of days," the woman said. She sounded resigned—like she had already given up on the goat.

"That it has," Anya agreed.

"We were in the shelter last night. Didn't sleep

a wink. Kept thinking we were going to lose everything," the woman continued. "But the house is still here. The barn's still here—well, mostly. We didn't lose any cows or pigs. After all that good fortune, I think we can afford to splurge on this one unlucky critter."

Anya broke into a slow grin. "Great. That's just great! Stella, get a blanket out of the truck. Let's get this goat to the clinic right away."

Stella ran to the truck and hurried back as quickly as she could. Gif helped Anya load the goat into the backseat.

Anya was buoyant. "That goat is going to be just fine," she told Stella. "I'm going to make him better than ever."

Stella sat next to him all the way to the clinic.

Cora was standing in the door as they drove up.

"We've just got one goat," Anya called to her. "It wasn't as bad as Rose thought."

"That's great!" Cora said.

But Stella noticed that her sister's smile faded quickly. Too quickly. Something was wrong.

Stella's stomach gave a nervous lurch. Was it Rufus?

Anya carried the goat up the steps.

Stella followed, and stopped next to Cora. "What's up?"

"We got a call about half an hour ago," Cora

said. "Sooty's owner. He got here about five minutes ago. I've been doing my best to stall. I thought you might want to say good-bye."

"Thanks, Cora."

• *13* •

Stella went straight to Exam One. Sooty was standing at the front of her cage—almost as if she were waiting.

"Hey, sweetie," Stella said, lifting her out. "I'm going to miss you." She gave the kitten a kiss on the nose. Then she marched bravely out into the waiting room.

There was only one person waiting. An enormous man dressed in leather pants and a black T-shirt. He had long, gray hair pulled into a ponytail and a gray beard. His forearms were covered with tattoos.

Stella recognized him. She'd seen him in the supermarket a few times. He'd always scared her a little.

"Is this your kitten?" Stella asked.

"Yup." The giant lumbered to his feet and held out his arms.

"Mew!" Sooty was eagerly scrambling out of Stella's hands.

The giant cradled her gently in his immense arms—making Sooty look ridiculously small. The kitten instantly began to purr.

Then Stella heard another noise. A sort of loud sucking. She looked up—and was surprised to see that the tattooed man was crying.

"You okay?"

Sniff. Sniff. "I—I guess the last two days are catching up with me."

"What happened?"

"My cabin burned down. I lost everything except my bike."

"Oh. I'm so sorry."

"Don't be! Finding Snowflake makes it much easier. And I never would have found her without you."

"You're welcome," Stella whispered. "Um—I've got to go now."

Stella didn't wait for a response. She just fled. She ran into the boarder room and threw herself down on the cot. She felt like pulling the covers over her head and hiding forever.

How come the mean biker man could cry—and she couldn't?

Because you don't have anything to cry about, Stella told herself. *You're worried, that's all.*

My house might have burned down.

Rufus may be dead.
But I don't know for sure.

It was just that . . . keeping your hopes up was exhausting.

Stella closed her eyes.

She . . . just . . . needed . . . a . . . break.

Time slowly passed.

Stella could hear things happening in the clinic. The phone ringing. Cora using the copier. Once someone came to the door of the boarder's room, but whoever it was backed away when they saw Stella lying there.

Probably thought she was sleeping.

She wasn't sleeping.

She was just resting. Being alone.

After a while, Stella heard Bertha's voice. And Anya's. Animal carriers being dragged around. Sounded as if another load of rescued animals had come in.

Stella thought about Rufus. But she just didn't have the energy to get her hopes up.

Now Cora's voice had joined the others.

And was that her mother's voice?

Where has she been all morning? Stella wondered. She hadn't seen Norma since the night before. In the middle of the night when they'd thought they'd have to evacuate.

Stella heard Cora shout. It sounded like a happy shout. And then there was a burst of laughter.

What was going on?

Stella opened her eyes. She got to her feet and rushed into the other room.

"Stella!" Bertha hollered. "I just came from your house. It's fine!"

"It didn't burn down?"

"Nope!"

"Then what about . . ." Stella let her voice trail off because she had just felt something on her hand. Something wet and wonderful.

Stella looked down—and right into Rufus's sweet, furry face. He panted up at her.

"Rufus!" Stella reached down and scooped him up into a hug.

"Arf!"

"Stella—I think you're squeezing him too hard," Norma said.

"I'll stop," Stella said. And she really wanted to. But it wasn't easy.

ANIMALS AND FIRE

Forest fires like the one described in this story really do happen. Wildlife is affected by more than three thousand forest fires each year. House fires are dangerous, too. Each year, many pets are killed or injured when their owners' houses catch on fire.

Forest fires

Most forest fires start when lightning strikes a tree or the ground. The rest are the result of arson, untended camp fires, tossed cigarette butts, sparks from chain saws, fireworks, and downed power lines.

In Montana, outdoor fires usually occur in

July and August when forests are hot and dry. Other parts of the country experience fire season at different times of the year, depending on the climate. For example, the winter is fire season in California; in Pennsylvania, most fires occur during spring and fall.

Forest fires are frightening. Most people who see TV images of trees burning probably wonder what happens to wild animals when forests go up in flames.

Scientists learned much of what they know about animals and forest fires during the summer of 1988 when eight huge fires burned in Yellowstone National Park. Extreme drought and high winds helped spread the fires over one-third of the park's 2.2 million acres, and made 1988 the worst Yellowstone fire season since President Theodore Roosevelt founded the park in 1872.

During the fires, millions of trees withered to blackened trunks and the smoke grew thick enough to be seen from outer space. Two firefighters lost their lives trying to control the fires. A fall snowstorm finally doused the flames.

Yet, amazingly, nearly all of the park's animals lived through the fires. The few animals that died suffered from smoke inhalation much like the raccoon in this story. The fire killed 257 of the park's 30,000 elk, 9 of the park's 2,000 bison, 4 deer, 2 black bears, 2 moose, plus numerous snakes and crawling insects. Some fish were poisoned when firefighters accidentally spilled fire retardant in a stream. But not one bald eagle, whooping crane, grizzly bear, or endangered animal of any kind died.

Some animals benefited from the fire. Hawks, eagles, and other birds of prey ate exceptionally well when mice, voles, and other rodents they hunted were suddenly left without cover.

Grazing animals didn't have it so easy. The winter following the fires, bison, elk, and deer had an unusually hard time finding food and many died of starvation. However, scientists didn't blame this die-off on the fire alone.

Before the fire there had been six mild winters in a row. This had caused the park's population of grazing animals to grow too big. Scientists felt that this winter die-off was a natural event.

The die-off helped other species. Eagles, ravens, magpies, coyotes, and grizzly bears fed on an abundant supply of carcasses during the winter. The following spring these species gave birth to larger than usual families. Spring was also a plentiful time for grazing animals as plants like fireweed grew in the fire-blackened areas. Birds benefited from the huge number of beetles and other insects that hatched out of the burned tree trunks. Seed-eating birds like pine siskins, Clark's nutcrackers, and red crossbills feasted on the millions of lodgepole seeds that rained down on each acre of burned forest. Birds like Mountain bluebirds and tree swallows made nests in the burned trees.

House fires

Nobody knows exactly how many pets die in house fires each year, but there are two important things to know about pets and fire: You should never go back into a burning building to find a pet. Preparing ahead can greatly increase your pet's chances of surviving.

Here are some ways you can prepare for a fire:

- Make sure you know how to escape a fire in your house. Find two exits from each room, especially bedrooms. Windows can serve as emergency exits. Choose a place to meet your family members. This place should be a safe distance away from the house. Practice getting out of the house through the various exits.

- Install smoke detectors near bedrooms, including in the room where your pet sleeps.
- Make sure your pets have collars with their identification and rabies tags. On the back of one or both of the tags, add the name and telephone number of a friend or relative who does not live with you.
- Note your pets' favorite hiding places so you can tell firefighters where to look for them.
- Obedience-train your dog so that he cooperates in an emergency.
- Introduce a neighbor to your pets in case a fire breaks out when you're not home.
- Prepare an emergency supply kit for your pets. Include some of your pet's favorite food and any medication your pet needs to stay healthy.
- After a fire, have a veterinarian check your animals. Pets can suffer from smoke inhalation, or have burns beneath their fur or feathers.

Do you have any more ideas about keeping animals safe during fires? Emily Costello, the author of the *Animal Emergency* series, would like to hear from you. Send her an e-mail at **emily@enarch-ma.com** or write to her care of HarperCollins Children's Books.